EATS
TASHA'S TEA HOUSE
CORGIVILLE
WILLIAMSBURG
RICHMOND
804-674-9351
Dills-Mary Organics

THE GREAT CORGIVILLE KIDNAPPING

by Tasha Tudor

Little, Brown and Company
Boston New York Toronto London

To Cyrus and Rebecca Harvey
and Piper

First Edition

Library of Congress Cataloging-in-Publication Data

Tudor, Tasha.
The great Corgiville kidnapping / by Tasha Tudor.—1st ed.
p. cm.
Summary: His instincts and his training as a part-time private investigator make Caleb Corgi suspicious of a band of raccoons, especially when Corgiville's prize rooster disappears.
ISBN 0-316-85583-9
[1. Dogs—Fiction. 2. Animals—Fiction. 3. Mystery and detective stories.] I. Title.
PZ7.T8228Gr 1997
[Fic]—dc21 96-45412

10 9 8 7 6 5 4 3 2 1

SC

Published simultaneously in Canada by Little, Brown & Company (Canada) Limited

Printed in Hong Kong

Caleb Corgi, though quite a young dog, had attended an outstanding college in the South, from which he had received his C.D.X. degree (Companion Dog of Excellence). Having then studied under Piper Harvey, head screener of visiting salesmen for the renowned firm of Appletree and Emlyn, in Woodstock, Connecticut, he was now a member of Trackers Unlimited, the well-known dog detective agency based in Corgiville.

It was July, and Caleb was writing a scholarly paper on "The Relationship of Common Scents to Crime."

12
T. TUDOR
96

On the side, he was doing some private investigating. His attention had been caught by a curious phenomenon. Recently he had observed an increase in the number of raccoons in town. Claiming to be merely visiting their friend Hiram Racky and intent only on sightseeing, they bought large quantities of goods from the local merchants. This was fine for trade, but somehow Caleb sensed that the masked visitors were up to no good. There was a feeling of secrecy and conspiracy in the air.

What mischief could those clever fellows be planning?

The question ran constantly through his head. His suspicions were deepened by, of all things, a trash can that he came upon outside of Horatio Rabbit's vegetable patch. The can was vibrating violently, obviously occupied by someone in a bad temper. Caleb paused to examine this curious sight.

When he tapped on the lid, a shocking volley of oaths greeted his ears. He then lifted the lid, whereupon an infuriated red squirrel squeezed out, the usually white rings around his eyes pink with indignation.

"However did you manage to shut yourself inside there?" asked Caleb.

"I didn't!" shrieked the squirrel. "Those #*#*#* [quite unprintable] raccoons put me in it—said I was spying on them. They're up to no good, those boys! Riddled with fleas, too, #*#*#* [no censor would allow it]! You'd better watch your henhouses!" And without even so much as a thank-you, he dashed off.

Caleb's curiosity was growing.

What could he have meant? he asked himself. *Something is definitely up! I'll make the rounds of the village and ask some questions!*

More puzzling facts soon came to light, particularly in the bookshop run by Miss Purrrrvis.

"Yes, ever so many raccoons have been in and bought books," said Miss Purrrrvis, "and all cookbooks, Mr. Caleb—cookbooks and two very expensive books on hot air balloons. I'm completely out of stock and must reorder for Christmas. You can't imagine what publishers are like about shipping on time," she purred.

Caleb's next stop was Megan's Market. It was not so easy to discuss sales of the past weeks there, as the market did a huge business and was always crowded with rabbits, cats, and corgis.

He did find out, though, from Miss Bunhilda Bunn, that she had sold unusually large amounts of poultry stuffing and sage, as well as at least a dozen bottles of costly *herbes de Provence,* to a group of touring raccoons. "And," she added, "half a carton of Knock-'Em-Stiff—you know how raccoons are troubled with fleas!"

Caleb thanked Miss Bunn, then went to the post office to see if any mail had come by the morning train.

"Yes, sir," said the postmistress. "Here's a letter for you, Mr. Caleb, all the way from Canada, too!"

Caleb took the letter, seated himself on the base of the Civil War statue, and proceeded to read it. It was from Charley Crow, an old college friend, who lived in Canning, Nova Scotia.

Charley had studied with Caleb on various questions—"The Art of Concealing Stolen Goods," for one. *Charley got an A+ on that one,* Caleb recalled. *Good old Charley!*

Charley wrote the usual news about wheat crops. Then he went on to say that there was great excitement among the Canadian raccoons about the plans of their leader, Zebulon Raccoon. Zebulon, the inventor of numberless brilliant trash can openers, was also justly famous for his skill in picking the locks of henhouse doors. And as if these achievements were not enough, Zebulon was the co-inventor, with Hiram Racky, of the Unbeatable Pie Extractor, used so successfully by raccoons on pantries throughout New England and Nova Scotia.

Charley's letter continued: "Z.R. is leaving Canada for an extended tour of New England and has asked 'yours truly' to cover the trip for the *Raccoon Radical*. So I'll be flying down tomorrow and hope to see you. I've got a lot of good undercover stuff to tell you! Yours, Charley."

"Aha!" said Caleb. "Things are beginning to fit together! Zebulon Raccoon is coming down here. The local raccoons will be planning a feast for him. Those raccoons ARE up to mischief. Poultry stuffing and sage! I must warn Mert to set a guard around Babe."

Babe was the famous "Biggest Rooster on Earth," who made a yearly sensation at the Corgiville Fair, bringing in huge gate receipts for the fair and for his owners. Babe was owned by a syndicate of boggarts. Originally from Sweden, boggarts have long tails and smoke cigars and are apt to be wild. Their hair is moss, their ears are leather, and their arms come off for convenience when going down holes. The boggarts that owned Babe were the olive green kind with spots. They took great pains to take good care of Babe. He was presently lodged in Mert Boggart's up-to-date poultry house at The Boggs.

Caleb lost no time in setting off for Mert's, but he was delayed by meeting Horatio Rabbit in a state of palpitations. Naturally he stopped to see what he could do for Horatio and asked what had brought on the condition.

"It was simply terrifying!" said Horatio.

"What was terrifying?"

"What I saw last night. Oh! It was DREADFUL!"

"But what was it you saw? Tell me!" said Caleb.

Horatio sat down and mopped his brow.

"I was coming home late last night, very late, from a meeting of the Ancient and Honorable Society of Hares, when I saw it! An EEEnormous flying object, Mr. Caleb, with a lurid glow under it. It was right overhead, and I was too frightened to do anything but dive into a haystack in Mert's meadow. It was fearful, REALLY fearful!" Horatio Rabbit's teeth began to chatter.

"Didn't you observe where it went?" asked Caleb. "It would help a great deal to know."

"No," Horatio said, "I was too frightened to do anything but hide."

"Well, if I were you, I would go and make yourself a super-strong cup of Appletree and Emlyn's rosehip tea. It should make you feel better. There's nothing like vitamin C for the nerves!"

Whereupon Caleb hurried on to Mert's with much on his mind and deploring the lack of spunk in rabbits in general.

As luck would have it, Mert was out. Caleb was dismayed. He left a note saying: “Urgent. Contact me at once! Serious! Caleb.”

He then turned homeward, after taking a look at Babe, who was luxuriously dust-bathing in a hole the size of a crater behind the henhouse. Babe winked at Caleb, closing one of his golden eyes voluptuously as the warm dust sifted through his feathers. "Delicious!" he murmured, and shut the other eye.

Caleb hurried on. *I must think out a plan of action,* he said to himself. It was all too obvious that the wily raccoons were up to some deviltry and that he, Caleb, must make an effort to circumvent their evil designs.

On reaching home, he ate three raw hamburgers and, exhausted with tension, dropped into the hammock. He dozed off but was brought back to reality by a hubbub of voices.

An excited crowd was coming up the road toward his house. Caleb's father, Mr. Bigby Brown, was one of Corgiville's leading citizens, always consulted in times of crisis. Everyone was talking at once. "Babe's gone! Babe's been kidnapped!"

Mr. Brown met the excited citizens at his gate. They confirmed the fact that Babe had indeed been kidnapped. The valuable bird had been spirited away so cleverly that not a trace or a hint or even a stray feather was to be found for a clue.

Babe simply had not been there when Mert had returned from town with six cans of Super Delousing Powder with which to dust the immense bird.

The citizens were very agitated. Some fights had even broken out, and the usual numbers of fainting rabbits were having to be revived.

Caleb heard the news with dismay.

"Too late! I'm too late!" He growled and clenched his handsome white teeth.

"But I'll make up for it!" And he dashed off to his father's office, where Mr. Brown was considering the situation.

"Let me handle this case, Dad—I guarantee I can rescue him! But it's a one-man operation—a posse could spell Babe's end. I've got clues that Hiram Racky's gang have him. Give me four hours, Dad, just four, and I swear I'll bring him back!"

Mr. Brown was confused, but he had a great deal of respect for his son and took great pride in him.

"All right," he said. "You slip off while I calm the crowd, but remember—four hours is the limit. After that we send a posse. Be careful, my son. This is not puppy stuff!"

Caleb gripped his father's paw with emotion and hurried off to prepare.

He grabbed his knapsack. Into it he put a watch, his knife, a flash-light, matches, a compass, a coil of rope, two chocolate bars, and a box of Liv-A-Snaps.

He then carefully applied OdorGone to his paws and behind his ears before quietly slipping out the back door, his jaw set.

He headed north toward Wayne's Pond, where Hiram Racky and his gang lived in a gigantic oak tree of great age. It was so old that, had it been in the right locality, George Washington could have bivouacked beneath it during the French and Indian Wars.

The day was warm, the way tortuous and long. Caleb's nerves were on edge. He wished he had given himself more time. The slightest noise caused him to pant. It was already close to noon as he approached the oak tree—11:55, to be exact.

A good time, he said to himself. *The raccoons should be taking their noon siesta. If I can look about a bit on the Q.T., I may discover Babe's whereabouts.*

He crept up, being careful to keep downwind, and concealed himself behind a stump that afforded him a good view of the oak's main entrance.

He had barely settled for the vigil when he became aware of voices coming from a hole partway up the stump. What luck! He realized that the stump was one of the many ventilators used to air the myriad passages, cells, storerooms, and dungeons that made up Hiram Racky's stronghold. Caleb pressed his ear to the opening. At first it was difficult to sort out what was being said, there were so many raccoons and all talking at once. And the smell of raccoon was simply fearful. It made Caleb's nose itch. He suppressed a sneeze.

A heated discussion was going on about the various methods of roasting and stuffing a large fowl. Several stuffings were up for choice. Some raccoons swore by the *Joy of Cooking*'s recipe; for others it was Julia Child's or nothing. One group wanted onion; another, breadcrumbs and sage.

Then Caleb heard a series of sharp raps calling the noisy meeting to order. The authoritative voice of Hiram Racky broke in.

“Too much time,” said Racky, clearing his throat, “is being taken up with these cooking details—I say this is mere woman’s work. What I think is more to the point is this: We should reward our two members who managed the brilliant coup of abducting the hulking rooster from under the very noses of the citizens of Corgiville, even outwitting the boggarts!”

Loud applause.

“My fellows in many crimes,” continued Racky, evidently addressing the two abductors, “I hereby award you the highest order of raccoon merit: the glorious Order of Mercury, the god of thieves.”

Wild applause. Several “Hear, hears!” and “Bravos!”

“Henceforth, the letters O.M. will follow your illustrious names. My profound congratulations!”

Wild cheering, stamping, clapping, and so forth.

“Now, our next move,” declared Racky, “will be to kill our victim and prepare him for roasting!”

Great licking of lips and even wilder clapping and stamping. But then the hubbub was broken off suddenly by another noise in the trees above Caleb’s head: a flock of blue jays screaming, “Fox! Fox! Fox!” all looking and gesturing at him, evidently having mistaken him for one of his woodland-dwelling cousins.

Quick as lightning, Caleb made a dash for safety, and only just in time. Dozens of raccoons poured out of holes in the oak, coming down backward, ready for trouble.

The jays, at the sight of so many agitated raccoons, promptly forgot Caleb and directed their screams at this new quarry. What a break!

But then Caleb thought his end had come: He tripped over a taut rope in a clump of hemlocks where he had thought to conceal himself. He fell flat, giving his chin a nasty whack. He just managed to retreat, undiscovered, to the shelter of some rocks that were covered by bushes.

He crouched among the rocks and bracken, his heart thumping so loudly, he was fearful the raccoons would hear it.

He could see the raccoons sniffing the air, their tails like bottlebrushes. He thanked his stars that he had taken thought to apply OdorGone to his paws. He noted that the raccoons seemed more concerned with examining the clump of hemlocks where he had tripped on the rope than searching farther afield.

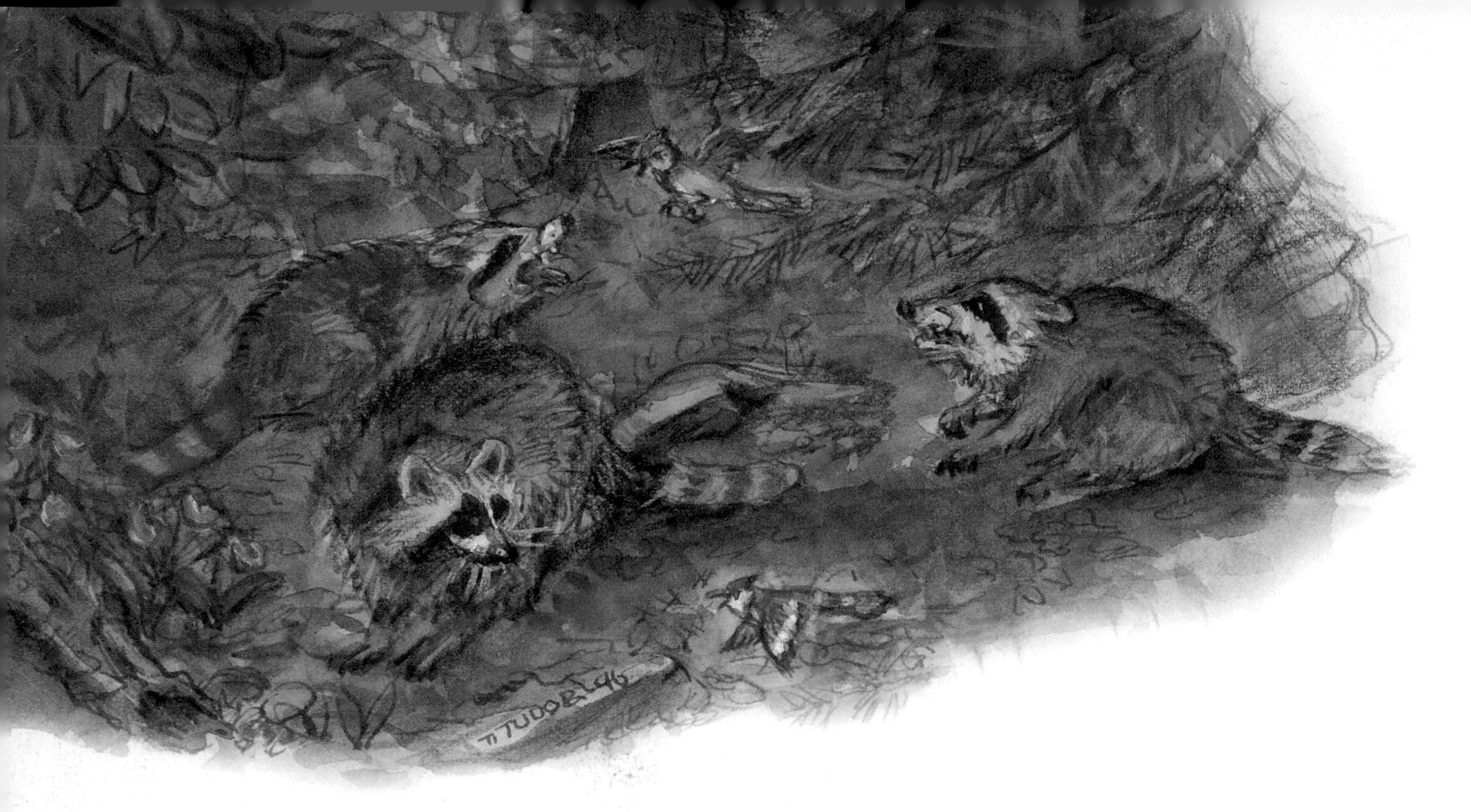

After bristling about for a while, the scouts returned to the oak, grumbling at having been diverted from their meeting by a false alarm. They returned to their stronghold, shaking their fists and saying crude things to the jays, who said equally crude things back before departing in search of an owl to tease.

Caleb heaved a sigh of relief and ate some Liv-A-Snaps to calm himself. It had been too dangerously close a call. All the while, the memory of the rope incident kept running through his mind.

I know that rope has something to do with Babe! I KNOW it has, it has, it has—I'm not Gertrude Stein, but she had something there—a rope is a rope . . . and at the end of that rope must be Babe!

Impatient to explore this new approach, he crawled through some tall ferns and made his way to the clump of hemlocks, his heart thumping wildly. Yes, there was a rope, and what was more, he now saw that there was a rope ladder dangling from above. In his haste and fright, he hadn't noticed it when he tripped. Looking up, he also made out a large nestlike object well above his head.

"That's where Babe is or I'm not a Welsh corgi!" he exclaimed, and, throwing caution to the winds, he spat on his paws, grasped the ladder, and climbed up.

Upon reaching what he had thought was a nest, he found it to be a large basket attached to a hot air balloon, well concealed by the dense hemlocks and tugging at the ropes that held it.

IN THE BASKET WAS BABE!!!

Yes, there he was, tied and gagged, his golden eyes squinting miserably.

Caleb foolishly let out a yelp of triumph. In no time flat, a horde of raccoons surged from the oak.

At this tense moment, Caleb felt a violent tremor on the rope ladder and, to his horror, saw a ferocious raccoon, a cutlass between his teeth, ascending on the double.

Caleb lost no time. He leaped into the basket, whipped out his knife, and cut the ropes! The balloon jumped skyward—but not before the agile pursuer grasped the rim, causing the basket to lurch sickeningly.

Caleb kept his head. In the split second he had taken to slash the ropes, his brain had registered the presence of a pressurized can of Knock-'Em-Stiff lying in the bottom of the basket. Instinctively he grabbed it and aimed it full in the face of the snarling raccoon, whose hot breath was now all too close. He pressed the button. The result was spectacular! The raccoon let out a yell of rage, lost his grip, and fell, crashing down upon his mates below, who had already been closing in for the kill!

Caleb sank back, limp with fear and relief. He could hear the bloodcurdling snarls of his enemies growing fainter and fainter as the balloon gained altitude. He relived in his mind the terrifying incident, the hairbreadth escape, the stroke of luck.

"If it hadn't been for the Knock-'Em-Stiff, Babe, we would have been in real trouble, and I don't mean maybe! Those raccoons must have been having mighty bad flea problems to have brought the can along in the first place! Whew! That was a lucky break for us!"

But now what? What, indeed?

Caleb realized that he should take stock of things. First he removed Babe's gag, much to the big bird's relief, as his gorgeous comb and wattles were becoming terribly numb. Caleb sensibly left Babe tied, knowing how easily chickens lose their heads. Next he examined the contents of the basket. In it were two crash helmets, two parachutes, some rope, a spyglass, and several large pumpkins, these last presumably for ballast.

For some time Caleb studied the confusing directions on how to affix the parachutes. After much head scratching, he managed to attach a parachute to himself and one to Babe. This last was quite a feat due to Babe's vast bulk.

He now peered over the edge of the basket in an attempt to discover where they were. He realized with dismay that, although the balloon was traveling south rapidly, it was at the same time losing altitude. Remembering *The Mysterious Island,* one of his favorite books, he proceeded to toss out weight, starting with the pumpkins.

Next went the two crash helmets, the rope, the spyglass, and the can of Knock-'Em-Stiff, though Caleb felt a twinge of regret in letting this go. He had wanted to keep it as a souvenir. The balloon rose a bit after this weight reduction, but now perversely headed for a church steeple some distance off. The steeple was topped by a large weather vane of shining copper in the shape of a rooster. Caleb could see Babe's hackles rising, and he was thankful he hadn't untied Babe, for the huge bird could easily become unmanageable.

The steeple loomed frighteningly close. Babe let out a mighty squawk and attempted to fling himself at what he took to be a rival. The basket gave a dreadful lurch and grazed the steeple, knocking off some slates and setting the weather vane askew, much to Babe's delight and Caleb's dismay. At the noise, an elderly cleric rushed from the church, followed by a group of committee ladies, all greatly alarmed. But to Caleb's immense relief, no pursuit was offered, and the balloon continued on at an increased rate of speed. A northwest wind had arisen, to add to their discomfort. The basket swayed and pitched. Caleb was distraught. It was past four o'clock. His time had run out. He didn't know how to manage the wild balloon, which was now leaping and dancing like a mad demon. He had begun to feel airsick. Furthermore, at any point, Babe could get out of hand.

"Let's get the old bird out first, and you follow. It's the best possible place to be dropped off before this gasbag crashes or goes out to sea."

Between them they untied Babe. The big rooster was feeling miffed at Charley's having called him an "old bird," but he was so glad to be untied that he kept quiet.

Charley and Caleb got him up and put the chute cord in his beak.

"Don't forget to pull it!" Caleb barked. "And don't crow."

With a flapping of wings, Babe leaped into space. The parachute opened perfectly and, due to the wind, kept pace with the racing balloon, which, relieved of Babe's weight, now doubled its speed and shot upward.

It was now Caleb's turn to jump. His senses swam. He closed his eyes, and his entire life sped through his mind like a film. He swallowed hard and leaped over the edge of the basket. He thought the chute would never open, but it did, and he sank closer to the welcoming earth, with Charley circling around and cawing encouragement. The balloon disappeared into the clouds as Caleb alighted on the roof of a warehouse. Babe came down close by, in an apple tree.

What was Caleb's astonishment when a skylight on the warehouse roof opened and out rushed his old teacher, Piper Harvey, who grasped his paw and exclaimed, "Whatever are you doing here, and in a parachute?" Caleb gave a rather disjointed account of what had happened, and then Piper, Charley, and Caleb went to Babe's assistance. Babe had managed to entangle himself and the parachute and the apple branches into one large snarl. It took quite a while to get him out and on his feet. He was weak with hunger.

Then they returned to the warehouse, which, of course, was Appletree and Emlyn's, and sent a telegram to Caleb's father in Corgiville saying that all was well. They gave Babe an entire tin of amaretto biscuits, which he ate greedily.

After this, they all repaired to Piper's house, where they ate an enormous supper. Babe spent the night in the sheep barn, though he had wanted to sleep in the garden house. At Caleb's mention of raccoons, however, he decided in favor of the barn and a hot bran mash, well laced with cayenne pepper.

Caleb went to bed early, but Piper and Charley sat up until midnight, Charley regaling Piper with his account of what had happened, adding several exaggerations to his own credit.

The following day, they returned to Corgiville, where a huge welcoming reception had been prepared. Caleb and Babe stood in line and shook paws and autographed innumerable slips of paper.

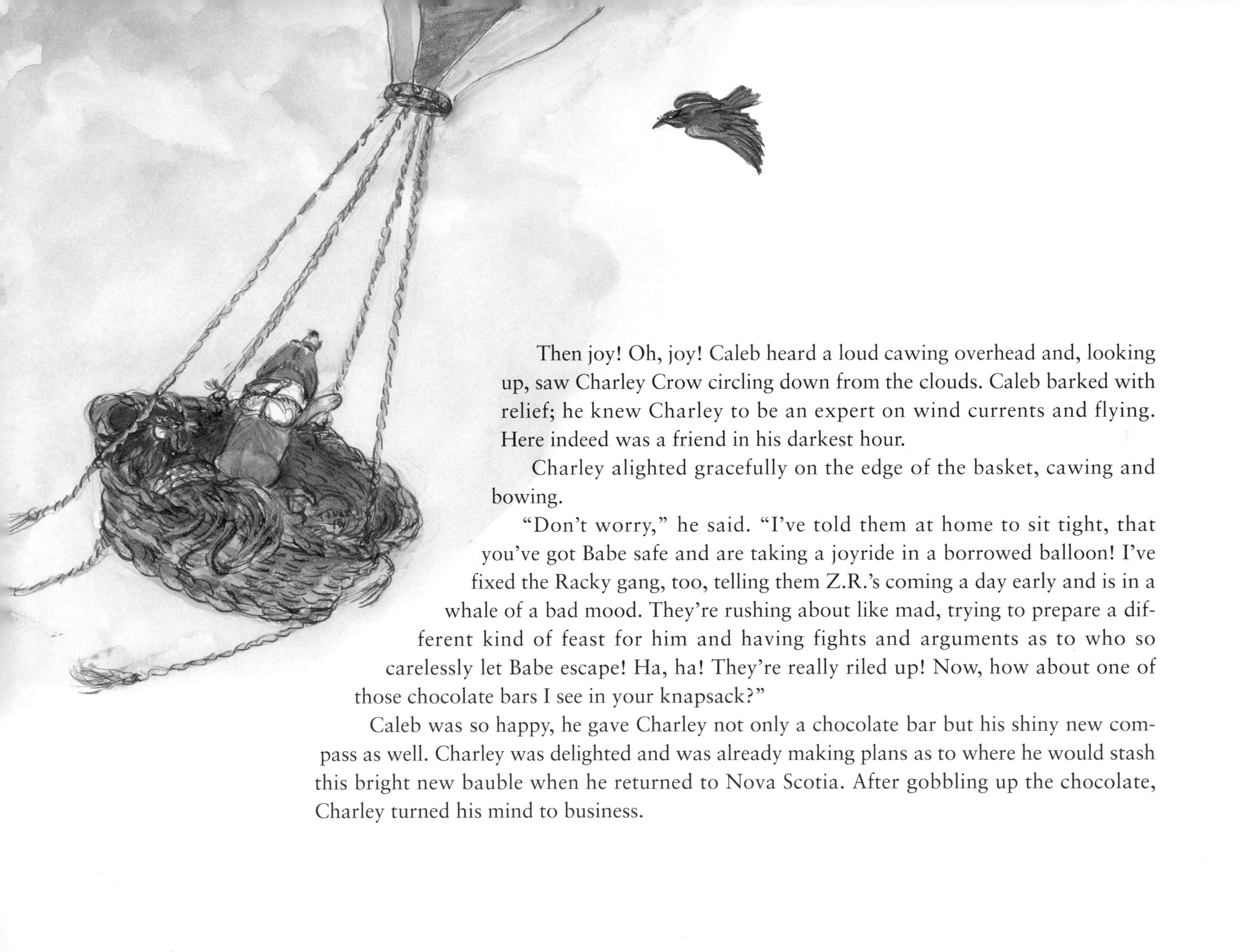

Then joy! Oh, joy! Caleb heard a loud cawing overhead and, looking up, saw Charley Crow circling down from the clouds. Caleb barked with relief; he knew Charley to be an expert on wind currents and flying. Here indeed was a friend in his darkest hour.

Charley alighted gracefully on the edge of the basket, cawing and bowing.

"Don't worry," he said. "I've told them at home to sit tight, that you've got Babe safe and are taking a joyride in a borrowed balloon! I've fixed the Racky gang, too, telling them Z.R.'s coming a day early and is in a whale of a bad mood. They're rushing about like mad, trying to prepare a different kind of feast for him and having fights and arguments as to who so carelessly let Babe escape! Ha, ha! They're really riled up! Now, how about one of those chocolate bars I see in your knapsack?"

Caleb was so happy, he gave Charley not only a chocolate bar but his shiny new compass as well. Charley was delighted and was already making plans as to where he would stash this bright new bauble when he returned to Nova Scotia. After gobbling up the chocolate, Charley turned his mind to business.

"We've got to get you free of this blasted windbag before it heads out to sea," Charley croaked.

Caleb shuddered but kept his fear under control.

"Are you prepared to jump?" was Charley's next question.

Caleb gulped but bravely said, "Yes!"

"Well, let's see where we are. Wow! That wind is really moving us! We'd better act quickly. I believe we're over Connecticut, northwestern part. I pass over it every fall on my way south to Philly." Caleb now looked at the scene below and realized that he recognized the area.

"Why, we're in Woodstock, Charley. Look, there's Piper Harvey's house, the big white one with the rock garden and the pond."

"Well, I'll be darned if you're not right!" said Charley.

According to Charley, the clever raccoons had managed to celebrate the arrival of their distinguished guest, Zebulon Raccoon, in spite of the fact that the pièce de résistance—roast Babe—was missing.

Instead, Charley assured him, the raccoons had put on a pie festival that was positively staggering. In fact, the housewives for miles around still claim that a band of rascally city boys had been on the loose stealing pies that week. But you can guess that it wasn't boys but those incredibly clever raccoons, wearing masks and using their Unbeatable Pie Extractors.

Babe, in his enthusiasm, started to pluck out feathers for his devoted fans, but Caleb soon put a stop to this, saying, "You don't want to look like an end-of-summer hen, do you?" Whereupon Babe's comb turned purple with embarrassment and no more feathers were offered.

Charley Crow was everywhere, taking photographs for his paper. Being an expert with cameras, Charley was far ahead of the other reporters in the field. Babe posed for him with numbers of puppies, young rabbits, and kittens on his broad back. Babe was a true politician. While posing, he entertained Charley with his version of how he had been kidnapped by the wily raccoons.

FAMOUS
ROOSTER
SAVED
BY
CALEB CORGI

TEA
POST